# Be Glad

## YOUR
## Nose
### IS ON YOUR
## Face

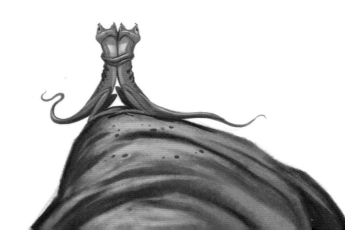

Some of the Best of Jack Prelutsky

# Be Glad

YOUR Nose

IS ON YOUR

Face

and other poems

*Illustrations by*

Brandon Dorman

Greenwillow Books

*An Imprint of HarperCollinsPublishers*

Library of Congress Cataloging-in-Publication Data

Prelutsky, Jack.
Be glad your nose is on your face and other poems :
some of the best of Jack Prelutsky / by Jack Prelutsky ;
illustrated by Brandon Dorman.
p. cm.
"Greenwillow Books."
Includes activities and indexes.
ISBN 978-0-06-157653-9 (trade bdg.)
1. Children's poetry, American.  I. Dorman, Brandon, ill.  II. Title.
PS3566.R36B33 2008    811'.54—dc22    2008013371

First Edition  10 9 8 7 6 5 4 3 2 1

 Greenwillow Books

To my wife, Carolynn, who makes it all possible
—J. P.

To my amazing wife, Emily, and to our children,
who bless my life with a smile each morning,
sunshine on rainy days, and laughter on evening walks
—B. D.

# Contents

# Introduction

For more than forty years Jack Prelutsky has been making me—and the children for whom he writes—laugh. And even more to the point, his wonderfully funny, silly, surprising, horrific, and brainy poems have been making us aware that language can be played with, that it can be fun. It is almost impossible to read a batch of Prelutsky poems without having one stick in your head, sometimes happily, sometimes maddeningly. For forty years I have found myself quoting (slightly incorrectly), "Hip-hop hoppity, hip-hop hoppity, the rabbit's ears are soft and floppity . . ." It is not great poetry. It is not even in this book. But it is in my head—forever.

Jack Prelutsky is a prime example of someone who has never gotten over being a child. I think he must remember each day, each meal, each embarrassment, and each triumph. That's why his poems resonate with children. He is one of them. Adults are sometimes put off by the very things that make the poems work: to us, eating worms, or eyeballs, or lizard dumplings is distinctly unappealing. Not so to a kid. Adults worry that Jack's ghouls and goblins and dragons are frightening. Kids have worse things to fear.

Jack plays with language the way most people play with Lego blocks. He puts things together that haven't been previously joined, but when you read them paired, they are inevitable. I think he must hear things differently from the rest of us. Certainly he knows things we don't. For instance, if you cross a spatula and a loon and create a creature called a Spatuloon, what would its call sound like? Jack apparently had no doubt: "Syrup! Syrup! Syrup!" Once you know, it is obvious. But could you have guessed? The logic is there, as it is in the twelve puns incorporated into "We're Fearless Flying Hot Dogs." On first reading, the three-stanza poem is a description of five acrobatic flying hot dogs. But in a more careful reading, one finds that they are "mustered" in formation, they fly with "relish," there is no "chilly" reception—and on and on, to a grand punning climax in which we learn that they are "the delicate essence" of flight. Jack is nothing if not generous. Any one of these throwaway jokes would have enriched the poem, but here they follow fast and furiously, to be discovered at the reader's leisure.

I think what I love best about Jack's poetry is that smug feeling of "of course" that one gets when one has been well and truly surprised by a poem, and realizes that the ending is built-in, however unforeseen it was. You read through "In the Cafeteria," in which the narrator begins a typical school food fight. But the final lines are "I believe that I am learning/What the food chain really means." Of course. You thought it was just a good poem about throwing stuff around. Now you have to think again.

Read "Is Traffic Jam Delectable?" on page 114. Or "Questions" on page 126. I can feel my mind beginning to work, my brain beginning to make its own connections. Jack doesn't ask the child to be creative—he takes it for granted that she will be. He swoops you up in his dance and gives you no option but to join in and have as good a time as he is having. It is contagious poetry, and it is worth catching.

A quick perusal of the poems in this collection turns up the words *evanescent, ominous, venerable, elusive, undulate, sombrous, scintillating, faze, mucilaginous,* and so many more. They taste good in the mouth. They sing in the poems. They are not there to "teach" but only to be enjoyed, like many small marshmallows in a mug of hot chocolate. Jack liked them—and so, he hopes, will you.

Food has always been of prime importance to Jack. Sometimes delicious food, sometimes unusual food, but always food worth reading about. As he says about one character (maybe himself?), "It eats what it wants and it always wants to eat." (Many years ago the only way I could think of to get Jack to write and deliver the poems for his next book was to promise him a weekly lunch in the Executive Dining Room in payment for a poem. It worked.) His use of food is highly original and always unexpected. The unlikely juxtaposition of the refrain "Sing a merry roundelay" in the poem glorifying "worm puree" just serves to make the main dish funnier—and more enticing. If you want a pail of eyeballs ("Delicious, nutritious"), here they are. And you can even have "Fierce dragon eyeballs/that cook by themselves." (As of course they would. But only Jack would have thought of it.) There is always a mind behind the combinations—thinking, playing, fooling, surprising—but never cheating, always being logical, always making its own unique sense.

Jack Prelutsky always carries a notebook with him, whether he is going hiking or out to dinner. He constantly jots down ideas for poems; beginnings, middles, or endings of poems; wordplays, game possibilities, names, anything that comes to mind that may be of use later on. The only time I ever saw him completely lose his cool was once when he had lost one of these notebooks in a New York taxi. It was subsequently returned, and I have always wondered what the finder thought when he looked inside. I wish I could have seen his face.

In 2006 Jack Prelutsky was named the first Children's Poet Laureate in the U.S. It was an honor for him—and for children as well. Taking his funny poems seriously, and giving them the respect they have long deserved, is also taking children seriously. And children and the very best of literature—both serious and humorous—belong together. I have been a Prelutsky fan for almost half a century. That thought makes me happy. But what makes me happier is knowing that Jack's poems will continue to be read and memorized and loved and laughed over long into the future. Like Mother Goose and Edward Lear and Lewis Carroll, Jack Prelutsky will make children giggle for generations to come. Like his own jiggling juggler, "he makes all things take magical wings." And once you are airborne with Prelutsky, you never know where you are going until you get there. That is his secret—and his genius.

—Susan Hirschman
*Jack Prelutsky's longtime editor*
*and the founder of Greenwillow Books*
2008

# A Letter from Jack Prelutsky

Dear Friends,

Welcome to *Be Glad Your Nose Is on Your Face*. When I wrote my first rhymes about imaginary animals more than forty years ago, I never dreamed that someday I'd have a book like this. As a matter of fact, it took me so long to write my first book of poems, *A Gopher in the Garden*—and even longer to get it published—that I never even thought I'd have a second book, let alone more than seventy.

I'm absolutely delighted that Greenwillow Books has given me the opportunity to assemble this hefty collection. It's filled with poems that I've selected from many of my other books, plus fifteen brand-new poems that I wrote especially for this book. I'm also delighted that the gifted artist Brandon Dorman, who illustrated *The Wizard*, was chosen to illustrate this book in full color.

Brandon is the latest of the many skilled illustrators that I've been so fortunate to work with. Some others are Arnold Lobel, Victoria Chess, James Stevenson, Marylin Hafner, Yossi Abolafia, Garth Williams, Paul O. Zelinsky, Peter Sís, Petra Mathers, Carin Berger, Doug Cushman, Chris Raschka, and Ted Rand. I know that I owe much of my success to these talented people, and I thank them all.

Poetry enriches lives. With that in mind, I encourage you to share the poems in this collection with your family and friends. Perhaps you and your family can even set aside a regular time to read poems together.

There are two bonuses in this book. First, there are fifteen activities, games, and puzzles that I dreamed up for you. And second, there is a CD on which I've recorded thirty of the poems, many of them to music. Enjoy, and keep reading!

Your friend,

Jack Prelutsky

Section One

# It's Hard
# to Be
# an Elephant

# The Egg

If you listen very carefully, you'll hear the chicken hatching.

At first there scarcely was a sound, but now a steady scratching;

and now the egg begins to crack, the scratching starts to quicken,

as anxiously we all await the exit of the chicken.

And now a head emerges from the darkness of the egg,

and now a bit of fluff appears, and now a tiny leg,

and now the chicken's out at last, he's shaking himself loose.

But, wait a minute, that's no chicken . . . goodness, it's a goose.

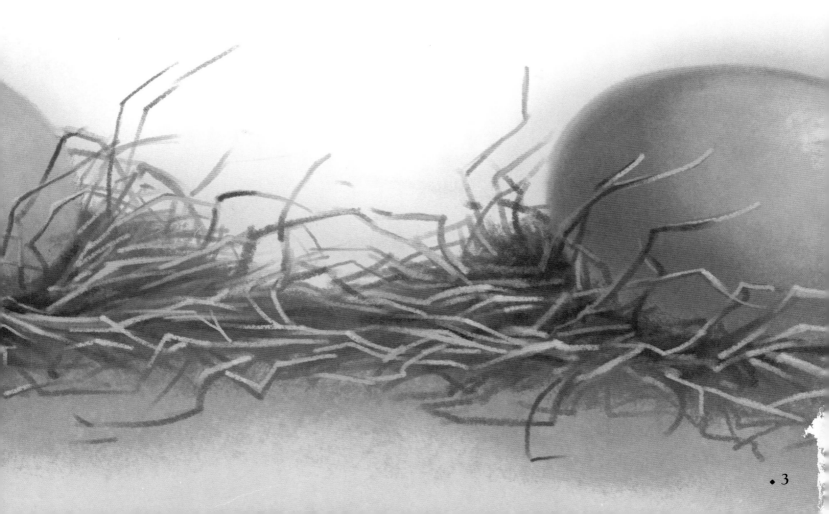

# We're Four Ferocious Tigers

We're four ferocious tigers,
at least, that's what we seem,
our claws are at the ready,
our sharp incisors gleam,
we're quite intimidating,
our stare will make you blink,
our roar will make you shiver,
at least, that's what we think.

We're four ferocious tigers,
at least, that's what we hear,
our ominous demeanor
will chill your atmosphere,
and yet you need not fear us,
don't scream and run away,
we only eat spaghetti,
at least, that's what we say.

# It's Hard to Be an Elephant

It's hard to be an elephant,
enormous, broad, and tall.
I can't attend the cinema,
the seats are all too small.
It's practically impossible
for me to board a bus,
the tires often flatten,
and the driver makes a fuss.

I'm ushered out of luncheonettes,
the waitresses are rude.
They fume, "We cannot feed you,
for you'll finish all our food."
I'm drawn to the piano,
but I'm daunted when I play,
I tend to be ungainly,
and my ears get in the way.

My trunk is far too powerful,
no sooner do I sneeze
than windows crack and shatter
from the impact of the breeze.
I'm plagued by a peculiar,
purely pachydermal plight—
I find no socks and underwear
that fit precisely right.

# Chitterchat

You may now make my acquaintance,
I am famous Chitterchat,
My old witch's dear familiar,
And a venerable cat.
I am steeped in ancient wisdom,
Rich in elemental lore,
Though my witch knows much of witching,
I'm replete with volumes more.

I'm no doddering grimalkin
Mystified by skeins of yarn,
Or some simple-minded mouser
Chasing shadows in a barn.
I'm no skulker in an alley,
Culling bones for bits of fish,
And no pampered portly feline
Lapping from a porcelain dish.

I've but little time to trifle
With such stuff as wool and mice,
For I'm sworn to guide my mistress
And provide her with advice.
If my witch omits essentials,
I discreetly show her how
To conduct her incantation—
It takes just the right meow!

# Brachiosaurus

Brachiosaurus had little to do
but stand with its head in the treetops and chew,
it nibbled the leaves that were tender and green,
it was a perpetual eating machine.

Brachiosaurus was truly immense,
its vacuous mind was uncluttered by sense,
it hadn't the need to be clever and wise,
no beast dared to bother a being its size.

Brachiosaurus was clumsy and slow,
but then, there was nowhere it needed to go,
if Brachiosaurus were living today,
no doubt it would frequently be in the way.

# Clankity Clankity

Clankity Clankity Clankity Clank!
Ankylosaurus was built like a tank,
its hide was a fortress as sturdy as steel,
it tended to be an inedible meal.

It was armored in front, it was armored behind,
there wasn't a thing on its minuscule mind,
it waddled about on its four stubby legs,
nibbling on plants with a mouthful of pegs.

Ankylosaurus was best left alone,
its tail was a cudgel of gristle and bone.
Clankity Clankity Clankity Clank!
Ankylosaurus was built like a tank.

# My Dog,
# He Is an Ugly Dog

My dog, he is an ugly dog,

he's put together wrong,

his legs are much too short for him,

his ears are much too long.

My dog, he is a scruffy dog,

he's missing clumps of hair,

his face is quite ridiculous,

his tail is scarcely there.

My dog, he is a dingy dog,

his fur is full of fleas,

he sometimes smells like dirty socks,

he sometimes smells like cheese.

My dog, he is a noisy dog,

he's hardly ever still,

he barks at almost anything,

his voice is loud and shrill.

My dog, he is a stupid dog,

his mind is slow and thick,

he's never learned to catch a ball,

he cannot fetch a stick.

My dog, he is a greedy dog,

he eats enough for three,

his belly bulges to the ground,

he is the dog for me.

# My Mouse Is Out

My mouse is out, my mouse is out,
it's scooting through the house.
It managed to escape its cage—
it's clever . . . for a mouse.
It waited till I went to bed,
then softly, while I slept,
it engineered its freedom . . .
it's ingenious and adept.

That rodent is resourceful,
and unwilling to be caught.
It's possibly the smartest mouse
that I have ever bought.
My sisters and my brothers
are assisting in the chase,
but my mouse is too elusive
as it darts from place to place.

So far our finest efforts
haven't been of any use.
My mouse is keen, and capable
of staying on the loose.
It's taking full advantage
of the fact that it's so small—
it's fled beneath the sofa,
where we cannot reach at all.

My mother's shrieking in alarm,
and bolting from the house.
"I won't be back," she's promising,
"until you catch that mouse."
I hope we catch it very soon,
though it's no easy chore,
for even though I love my mouse,
I love my mother more.

# If Not for the Cat

If not for the cat,

And the scarcity of cheese,

I could be content.

# Boneless, Translucent

Boneless, translucent,
We undulate, undulate,
Gelatinously.

◆ 19

# The Frogs Wore Red Suspenders

The frogs wore red suspenders
and the pigs wore purple vests,
as they sang to all the chickens
and the ducks upon their nests.

They croaked and oinked a serenade,
the ducks and chickens sighed,
then laid enormous spangled eggs,
and quacked and clucked with pride.

# My Frog Does Not Waste Precious Time

My frog does not waste precious time
just sitting on a log.
He's learned to use the Internet,
and now he has a blog.
It's filled with tips on how to hop,
and how to catch a fly,
on things that frogs can do to keep
their skins from getting dry.

My frog has hints on where to find
the finest lily pads,
and writes in great detail about
the latest froggy fads.
He tells of different ways to croak,
and how to act in bogs . . .
it's boring for most people,
but it fascinates most frogs.

# I Saw a Brontosaurus

I saw a brontosaurus
saunter through my neighborhood,
this struck me as peculiar,
as I'd heard they'd gone for good,
its proportions were imposing,
it was long and tall and wide,
I ran home to fetch a ladder,
then ascended for a ride.

It was hard to sit astride it,
for its hide was rather rough
and I had to ride it bareback,
there's no saddle big enough,
it turned in to the sunset
and we started heading west,
my parents seemed uneasy,
but the neighbors looked impressed.

We squeezed between the buildings
as we thundered out of town,
the beast became rambunctious,
and it bounded up and down,
it ignored my agitation
and my frequent shouts of "Whoa!"
and I almost bounced to pieces
as we crossed a wide plateau.

That brontosaurus tossed me
in the middle of a plain,
I landed in a wheat field,
where I fell against the grain,
though I treasure my adventure,
I won't do it anymore,
for that bucking brontosaurus
made my bottom brontosore!

# The Armadillo

The ancient armadillo
is as simple as the rain,
he's an armor-plated pillow
with a microscopic brain.

He's disinterested thoroughly
in what the world has wrought,
but spends his time in contemplative,
armadyllic thought.

# My Dog in Most Ways

My dog in most ways is the best.
In one way he's the worst—
he licks my face, but frequently
drinks from the toilet first.

P.S.
I wish he'd find another way
to satisfy his thirst.

# Ballad of a Boneless Chicken

I'm a basic boneless chicken,
yes, I have no bones inside,
I'm without a trace of rib cage,
yet I hold myself with pride,
other hens appear offended
by my total lack of bones,
they discuss me impolitely
in derogatory tones.

I am absolutely boneless,
I am boneless through and through,
I have neither neck nor thighbones,
and my back is boneless too,
and I haven't got a wishbone,
not a bone within my breast,
so I rarely care to travel
from the comfort of my nest.

I have feathers fine and fluffy,
I have lovely little wings,
but I lack the superstructure
to support these splendid things.
Since a chicken finds it tricky
to parade on boneless legs,
I stick closely to the hen house,
laying little scrambled eggs.

# My Dog May Be a Genius

My dog may be a genius,
and in fact, there's little doubt.
He recognizes many words,
unless I spell them out.
If I so much as whisper *"walk,"*
he hurries off at once
to fetch his leash . . . it's evident
my dog is not a dunce.

I can't say *"food"* in front of him,
I spell *f-o-o-d,*
and he goes wild unless I spell
his *t-r-e-a-t.*
But recently this tactic
isn't working out too well.
I think my *d-o-g* has learned
to *s-p-e-l-l.*

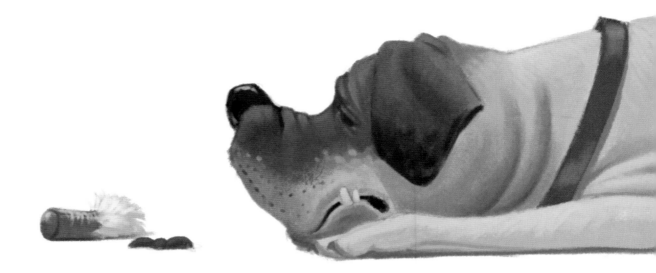

# Hello! How Are You? I Am Fine!

**Hello! How are you? I am fine!**

is all my dog will say,

he's probably repeated it

a thousand times today.

He doesn't bark his normal bark,

he doesn't even whine,

he only drones the same **Hello!**

**How are you? I am fine!**

**Hello! How are you? I am fine!**

His message doesn't change,

it's gotten quite monotonous,

and just a trifle strange.

**Hello! How are you? I am fine!**

It makes the neighbors stare,

they're unaware that yesterday

he ate my talking bear.

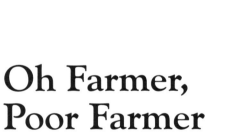

# Oh Farmer, Poor Farmer

Oh farmer, poor farmer, you're surely forlorn,
the crows have flown off with your Iowa corn,
they know your old scarecrow is nothing but straw,
they're feasting and boasting in chorus, "Caw! Caw!"

# Eleven Yellow Monkeys

Eleven yellow monkeys
in purple pantaloons
went to western Oregon
to play upon the dunes,
they whirled in dizzy circles
until they could not stand,
then grabbed each other by the tail
and tumbled in the sand.

Eleven yellow monkeys
wrestled for a while,
they tried a game of leapfrog
and landed in a pile,
by evening they grew weary,
and resting from their fun,
eleven yellow monkeys sat
and watched the setting sun.

# Here
# Come the Elephants

Here come the elephants, ten feet high,
elephants, elephants, heads in the sky.
Eleven great elephants intertwined,
one little elephant close behind.

Elephants over and elephants under,
elephants bellow with elephant thunder.
Up on pedestals elephants hop,
elephants go and elephants stop.

Elephants quick and elephants slow,
elephants dancing to and fro.
Elephants, elephants twice times six,
elephants doing elephant tricks.

Elephants strutting, elephants strolling,
rollicking elephants frolicking, rolling.
Elephants forming an elephant arch,
elephants marching an elephant march.

Elephants there and elephants here,
elephants cheering an elephant cheer.
Elephants, elephants, trunks unfurled,
in a wonderful, elegant elephant world.

# I'm Dancing with My Elephants

I'm dancing with my elephants,
a scintillating treat.
They're both extremely graceful,
light and limber on their feet.
They move with ease and elegance
and glide across the floor.
I'm dancing with my elephants . . .
how could I ask for more?

They effortlessly pirouette,
then leap into the air.
A crowd looks on in wonder
at this sight beyond compare.
And when they spin and somersault,
the crowd erupts and roars.
I'm dancing with my elephants—
I hope you dance with yours.

# Oh Sleek Bananaconda

Oh sleek BANANACONDA,
You longest long long fellow,
How sinuous and sly you are,
How slippery, how yellow.

You slither on your belly,
And you slither on your chin.
You're only unappealing
As you shed your slinky skin.

**buh-na-nuh-CON-duh**

# The Ballpoint Penguins

The BALLPOINT PENGUINS, black and white,

Do little else but write and write.

Although they've nothing much to say,

They write and write it anyway.


The BALLPOINT PENGUINS do not think,

They simply write with endless ink.

They write of ice, they write of snow,

For that is all they seem to know.


At times, these shy and silent birds

Will verbally express their words.

But mostly they do not recite—

They aim their beaks and write and write.


ball-point PEN-gwinz

# The Detested Radishark

In the middle of the ocean,
In the deep deep dark,
Dwells a monstrous apparition,
The detested RADISHARK.
It's an underwater nightmare
That you hope you never meet,
For it eats what it wants,
And it always wants to eat.

Its appalling, bulbous body
Is astonishingly red,
And its fangs are sharp and gleaming
In its huge and horrid head,
And the only thought it harbors
In its small but frightful mind,
Is to catch you and to bite you
On your belly and behind.

It is ruthless, it is brutal,
It swims swiftly, it swims far,
So it's guaranteed to find you
Almost anywhere you are.
If the RADISHARK is near you,
Pray the beast is fast asleep
In the middle of the ocean
In the dark dark deep.

**RAD-ish-ark**

# The Clocktopus

Emerging from the salty sea,
A wondrous beast appears.
It clearly is a CLOCKTOPUS,
We marvel as it nears.
It moves with slow precision
At a never-changing pace,
Its tentacles in tempo
With the clock upon its face.

While undulating east to west
Across the swirling sand,
It ticks away the minutes,
And it has a second hand.
We watch it for an hour
And it never goes astray—
There's nothing like a CLOCKTOPUS
To tell the time of day.

**CLOCK-tuh-puss**

# The Solitary Spatuloon

At home within a blue lagoon,
The solitary SPATULOON
Calls longingly as it glides by—
"Syrup!" is its plaintive cry.
The fowl, both curious and rare,
Now flips a pancake in the air.
Its tail, we note, is well designed
With this peculiar task in mind.

We watch with wonder and delight,
Until it vanishes from sight.
Yet, even as it disappears,
Faint strains of "Syrup!" fill our ears.
We wait, and as we wait we yearn,
In hopes the bird will soon return.
But sadly, in the blue lagoon,
We fail to spy the SPATULOON.

spat-chew-LOON

# Early One Morning on Featherbed Lane

Early one morning on Featherbed Lane,
I saw a white horse with a strawberry mane,
I jumped on his back just as fast as I could,
and we galloped away to the green willow wood.

We galloped all morning with never a stop,
where mockingbirds whistle and ladybugs hop,
we drank from a stream where the water runs free,
and we slept in the shade of a green willow tree.

# Activities

## My Frog Does Not Waste Precious Time

I have several hobbies. One of them is collecting frogs. Not real ones but little statuettes, made of just about any material you can think of. Because I'm so fond of these amphibians, I dreamed up a little game for you. I've hidden exactly seventeen frogs that look like this one throughout the book. I warn you, every frog doesn't count—only the ones that look like this, with a hat and a bowtie. They may be very small and be especially hard to find. Can you locate them all?

## Here Come the Elephants

There's something special about elephants, and I've written a number of poems about them. In my poem "Here Come the Elephants," I use the word *elephant* (or *elephants*) thirty-three times. Can you find thirty-three words of four or five letters by using the letters E—L—E—P—H—A—N—T? You can use the letter E twice in your words, since that letter appears twice in the word *elephant*. The other letters may be used only once per word. I've found forty-seven words so far. Maybe you can do even better. But if you find at least thirty-three words, I congratulate you.

## Scranimals and Umbrellaphants

In this book I've included several poems from my books *Scranimals* and *Behold the Bold Umbrellaphant*. "Scranimals" (a word I invented) are animals combined with fruits, vegetables, trees, flowers, and other living things. The "bananaconda" is a combination of *banana* and *anaconda*, and the "radishark" is a combination of *radish* and *shark*.

I created "umbrellaphants" (another invented word) by combining the names of animals with ordinary inanimate objects. The "clocktopus" is a combination of *clock* and *octopus*, and the "spatuloon" is a combination of *spatula* and *loon*.

How many of your own "scranimals" and "umbrellaphants" can you invent? Can you create ten of each? Take your time and have fun. Draw pictures of your imaginary creatures. If you're really ambitious, you might try writing poems about some of your fanciful creations.

*Answers on page 192.*

Section Two

# Oh Breakfast, Lovely Breakfast

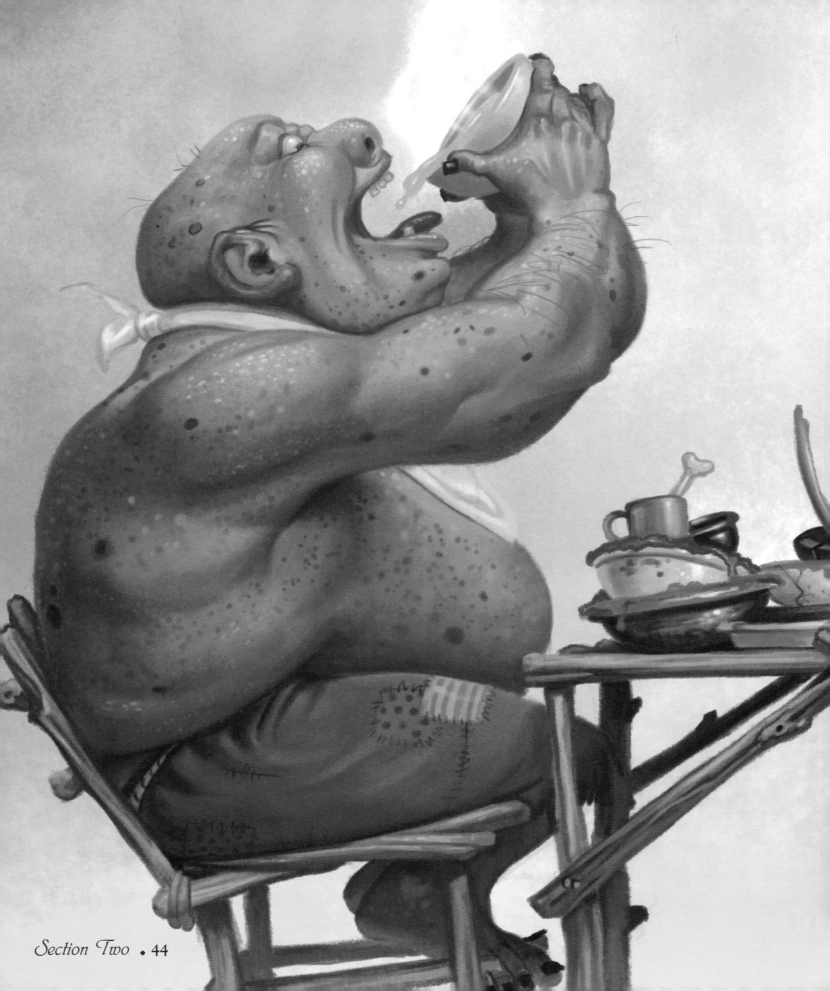

# Awful Ogre's Breakfast

Oh breakfast, lovely breakfast,
You're the meal I savor most.
I sip a bit of gargoyle bile
And chew some ghoul on toast.

I linger over scrambled legs,
Complete with pickled feet,
Then finish with a piping bowl
Of steamy SCREAM OF WHEAT.

# Bleezer's Ice Cream

I am Ebenezer Bleezer,

I run BLEEZER'S ICE CREAM STORE,

there are flavors in my freezer

you have never seen before,

twenty-eight divine creations

too delicious to resist,

why not do yourself a favor,

try the flavors on my list:

COCOA MOCHA MACARONI

TAPIOCA SMOKED BALONEY

CHECKERBERRY CHEDDAR CHEW

CHICKEN CHERRY HONEYDEW

TUTTI-FRUTTI STEWED TOMATO

TUNA TACO BAKED POTATO

LOBSTER LITCHI LIMA BEAN

MOZZARELLA MANGOSTEEN

ALMOND HAM MERINGUE SALAMI

YAM ANCHOVY PRUNE PASTRAMI

SASSAFRAS SOUVLAKI HASH

SUKIYAKI SUCCOTASH

BUTTER BRICKLE PEPPER PICKLE

POMEGRANATE PUMPERNICKEL

PEACH PIMENTO PIZZA PLUM

PEANUT PUMPKIN BUBBLEGUM

BROCCOLI BANANA BLUSTER

CHOCOLATE CHOP SUEY CLUSTER

AVOCADO BRUSSELS SPROUT

PERIWINKLE SAUERKRAUT

COTTON CANDY CARROT CUSTARD

CAULIFLOWER COLA MUSTARD

ONION DUMPLING DOUBLE DIP

TURNIP TRUFFLE TRIPLE FLIP

GARLIC GUMBO GRAVY GUAVA

LENTIL LEMON LIVER LAVA

ORANGE OLIVE BAGEL BEET

WATERMELON WAFFLE WHEAT

I am Ebenezer Bleezer,

I run BLEEZER'S ICE CREAM STORE,

taste a flavor from my freezer,

you will surely ask for more.

# My Mother
# Made a
# Meat Loaf

My mother made a meat loaf
that provided much distress,
she tried her best to serve it,
but she met with no success,
her sharpest knife was powerless
to cut a single slice,
and her efforts with a cleaver
failed completely to suffice.

She whacked it with a hammer,
and she smacked it with a brick,
but she couldn't faze that meat loaf,
it remained without a nick,
I decided I would help her
and assailed it with a drill,
but the drill made no impression,
though I worked with all my skill.

We chipped at it with chisels,
but we didn't make a dent,
it appeared my mother's meat loaf
was much harder than cement,
then we set upon that meat loaf
with a hatchet and an ax,
but that meat loaf stayed unblemished
and withstood our fierce attacks.

We borrowed bows and arrows,
and we fired at close range,
it didn't make a difference,
for that meat loaf didn't change,
we beset it with a blowtorch,
but we couldn't find a flaw,
and we both were flabbergasted
when it broke the power saw.

We hired a hippopotamus
to trample it around,
but that meat loaf was so mighty
that it simply stood its ground,
now we manufacture meat loaves
by the millions, all year long,
they are famous in construction,
building houses tall and strong.

# Worm Puree

*Worm puree, oh hooray!*
*You're the dish that makes my day.*
*Sing a merry roundelay.*
*Worm puree, hooray!*

Worm puree, I must say,
you're divine in every way.
Hot or cold, fresh or old,
I'm your devotee.

*Worm puree, oh hooray!*
*You're the dish that makes my day.*
*Sing a merry roundelay.*
*Worm puree, hooray!*

Worms with rice, oh so nice,
every forkful, every slice.
When I chew bits of you,
I'm in paradise.

*Worm puree, oh hooray!*
*You're the dish that makes my day.*
*Sing a merry roundelay.*
*Worm puree, hooray!*

Worms with cheese, mashed with peas,
you are guaranteed to please.
Every bite is delight,
and slides down with ease.

*Worm puree, oh hooray!*
*You're the dish that makes my day.*
*Sing a merry roundelay.*
*Worm puree, hooray!*

Worm puree, pink and gray,
you're a heavenly entree.
Just one spoon makes me swoon,
worm puree, hooray!

*Worm puree, oh hooray!*
*You're the dish that makes my day.*
*Sing a merry roundelay.*
*Worm puree, hooray!*

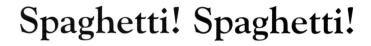

# Spaghetti! Spaghetti!

Spaghetti! spaghetti!
you're wonderful stuff,
I love you, spaghetti,
I can't get enough.
You're covered with sauce
and you're sprinkled with cheese,
spaghetti! spaghetti!
oh, give me some please.

Spaghetti! spaghetti!
piled high in a mound,
you wiggle, you wriggle,
you squiggle around.
There's slurpy spaghetti
all over my plate,
spaghetti! spaghetti!
I think you are great.

Spaghetti! spaghetti!
I love you a lot,
you're slishy, you're sloshy,
delicious and hot.
I gobble you down
oh, I can't get enough,
spaghetti! spaghetti!
you're wonderful stuff.

# Song of the Lizard Lovers

*Lizard, oh lizard, we love you, we do.*
*There's no finer reptile to nibble or chew.*
*No toad ever tickled our taste buds like you.*
*Lizard, oh lizard, we love you, we do.*

We love eating lizard, so savory and sweet.
A meal without lizard is quite incomplete.
We love lizard sizzled in onions and oil,
we love lizard simmered, or brought to a boil.

*Lizard, oh lizard, we love you, we do.*
*There's no finer reptile to nibble or chew.*
*No toad ever tickled our taste buds like you.*
*Lizard, oh lizard, we love you, we do.*

We love lizard gizzard, we love lizard legs,
we love lizard pickled, or scrambled with eggs.
We love lizard casserole, lizard on rye,
tongue of raw lizard still stuck to a fly.

*Lizard, oh lizard, we love you, we do.*
*There's no finer reptile to nibble or chew.*
*No toad ever tickled our taste buds like you.*
*Lizard, oh lizard, we love you, we do.*

We love munching lizard with carrots and peas,
slathered with ketchup, or dripping with cheese.
We love lizard dumplings, and lizard flambé . . .
there's nothing like lizard to brighten our day.

*Lizard, oh lizard, we love you, we do.*
*There's no finer reptile to nibble or chew.*
*No toad ever tickled our taste buds like you.*
*Lizard, oh lizard, we love you, we do.*

# Pumberly Pott's Unpredictable Niece

Pumberly Pott's unpredictable niece
declared with her usual zeal
that she would devour, by piece after piece,
her uncle's new automobile.

She set to her task very early one morn
by consuming the whole carburetor;
then she swallowed the windshield, the headlights and horn,
and the steering wheel just a bit later.

She chomped on the doors, on the handles and locks,
on the valves and the pistons and rings;
on the air pump and fuel pump and spark plugs and shocks,
on the brakes and the axles and springs.

When her uncle arrived she was chewing a hash
made of leftover hoses and wires
(she'd just finished eating the clutch and the dash
and the steel-belted radial tires).

"Oh what have you done to my auto," he cried,
"you strange unpredictable lass?"
"The thing wouldn't work, Uncle Pott," she replied,
and he wept, "It was just out of gas."

# My Mother Says I'm Sickening

My mother says I'm sickening,
my mother says I'm crude,
she says this when she sees me
playing Ping-Pong with my food,
she doesn't seem to like it
when I slurp my bowl of stew,
and now she's got a list of things
she says I mustn't do—

DO NOT CATAPULT THE CARROTS!
DO NOT JUGGLE GOBS OF FAT!
DO NOT DROP THE MASHED POTATOES
ON THE GERBIL OR THE CAT!
NEVER PUNCH THE PUMPKIN PUDDING!
NEVER TUNNEL THROUGH THE BREAD!
PUT NO PEAS INTO YOUR POCKET!
PLACE NO NOODLES ON YOUR HEAD!
DO NOT SQUEEZE THE STEAMED ZUCCHINI!
DO NOT MAKE THE MELON OOZE!
NEVER STUFF VANILLA YOGURT
IN YOUR LITTLE SISTER'S SHOES!
DRAW NO FACES IN THE KETCHUP!
MAKE NO LITTLE GRAVY POOLS!

I wish my mother wouldn't make
so many useless rules.

# Eyeballs for Sale!

Eyeballs for sale!
Fresh eyeballs for sale!
Delicious, nutritious,
not moldy or stale.
Eyeballs from manticores,
ogres, and elves,
fierce dragon eyeballs
that cook by themselves.

Eyeballs served cold!
Eyeballs served hot!
If you like eyeballs,
then this is the spot.
Ladle a glassful,
a bowlful, or pail—
Eyeballs! Fresh eyeballs!
Fresh eyeballs for sale!

# Willie Ate a Worm

Willie ate a worm today,
a squiggly, wiggly worm.
He picked it up
from the dust and dirt
and wiped it off
on his brand-new shirt.
Then slurp, slupp
he ate it up,
yes Willie ate a worm today,
a squiggly, wiggly worm.

Willie ate a worm today,
he didn't bother to chew,
and we all stared
and we all squirmed
when Willie swallowed
down that worm.
Then slupp, slurp
Willie burped,
yes Willie ate a worm today,
I think I'll eat one too.

# The Frummick and the Frelly

The frummick and the frelly
sat beneath a silver sky,
spreading jingleberry jelly
over pinkadoodle pie.

The frelly weighed a hundred tons,
the frummick matched its size.
They both ate bales of boiling buns
and countless piles of pies.

The frelly and the frummick
were in fairly mellow moods
as they stuffed their massive stomachs
with a great array of foods.

They fared on pairs of pickled yare
and shared a score of sneel.
They gorged on gare both burnt and rare
in their exotic meal.

They ate a clutch of candied snutch
and troves of tasty troove
in such a way they ate so much
that they could barely move.

And in that way, for quite some while,
the weighty couple sat,
each seeming, in its special style,
contented, full, and fat.

"There's nothing left to eat, dear friend,"
the frelly said at last.
"I fear our feast is at an end,
and such a fine repast."

"Ah fine, so fine," the frummick sighed
and scratched its bulging belly,
then opened wide and stuffed inside
the flabbergasted frelly.

# In the Cafeteria

I was feeling sort of silly,
So I took a bit of bread
And directed it precisely
At my buddy Benny's head.
"Who *did* that?" Benny shouted,
As he shot out of his seat,
Flinging carrots at Carlotta,
Who then threw her peas at Pete.

Pete took a small tomato wedge
And hurled it at Denise,
Who responded, catapulting
Macaroni at Felice.
Felice, whose aim is perfect,
Started pelting me with beans—
I believe that I am learning
What the food chain *really* means.

# Herbert Glerbett

Herbert Glerbett, rather round,
swallowed sherbet by the pound,
fifty pounds of lemon sherbet
went inside of Herbert Glerbett.

With that glop inside his lap
Herbert Glerbett took a nap,
and as he slept, the boy dissolved,
and from the mess a thing evolved—

a thing that is a ghastly green,
a thing the world had never seen,
a puddle thing, a gooey pile
of something strange that does not smile.

Now if you're wise, and if you're sly,
you'll swiftly pass this creature by,
it is no longer Herbert Glerbett.
Whatever it is, do not disturb it.

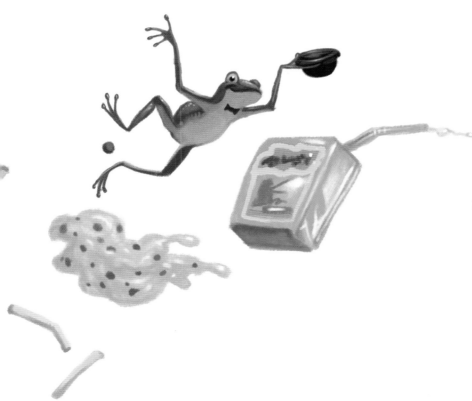

# A Pizza the Size of the Sun

I'm making a pizza the size of the sun,
a pizza that's sure to weigh more than a ton,
a pizza too massive to pick up and toss,
a pizza resplendent with oceans of sauce.

I'm topping my pizza with mountains of cheese,
with acres of peppers, pimentos, and peas,
with mushrooms, tomatoes, and sausage galore,
with every last olive they had at the store.

My pizza is sure to be one of a kind,
my pizza will leave other pizzas behind,
my pizza will be a delectable treat
that all who love pizza are welcome to eat.

The oven is hot, I believe it will take
a year and a half for my pizza to bake.
I hardly can wait till my pizza is done,
my wonderful pizza the size of the sun.

# Rat for Lunch!

*Rat for lunch! Rat for lunch!*
*Yum! Delicious! Munch munch munch!*
*One by one or by the bunch—*
*Rat, oh rat, oh rat for lunch!*

Scrambled slug in salty slime
is our choice at breakfast time,
but for lunch, we say to you,
nothing but a rat will do.

*Rat for lunch! Rat for lunch!*
*Yum! Delicious! Munch munch munch!*
*One by one or by the bunch—*
*Rat, oh rat, oh rat for lunch!*

For our snack each afternoon,
we chew bits of baked baboon,
curried squirrel, buttered bat,
but for lunch it must be rat.

*Rat for lunch! Rat for lunch!*
*Yum! Delicious! Munch munch munch!*
*One by one or by the bunch —*
*Rat, oh rat, oh rat for lunch!*

In the evening we may dine
on fillet of porcupine,
buzzard gizzard, lizard chops,
but for lunch a rat is tops.

*Rat for lunch! Rat for lunch!*
*Yum! Delicious! Munch munch munch!*
*One by one or by the bunch —*
*Rat, oh rat, oh rat for lunch!*

Rat, we love you steamed or stewed,
blackened, broiled, or barbecued.
Pickled, poached, or fried in fat,
there is nothing like a rat.

*Rat for lunch! Rat for lunch!*
*Yum! Delicious! Munch munch munch!*
*One by one or by the bunch —*
*Rat, oh rat, oh rat for lunch!*

# Percy's Perfect Pies

I am Percival P. Puffinwuff,
a baker of renown,
justly famous for creating
the most tasty pies in town.
I make pies for all occasions,
many flavors, any size,
here's a savory assortment
served at **Percy's Perfect Pies.**

PUMPKIN PANDA CORIANDER

CASSOWARY CURDLED CREAM

SALSA SALMON SALAMANDER

SKUNK ASPARAGUS SUPREME

MANGO KANGAROO VANILLA

MINNOW MARROW MARZIPAN

CHICKEN CHICKADEE CHINCHILLA

GNU MERINGUE ORANGUTAN

GOUDA GUPPY GOPHER GRISTLE

APPLE CAPPUCCINO RAT

SUSHI GOULASH THRUSH AND THISTLE

PHILODENDRON FERRET FAT

WEEVIL JELLY VERMICELLI

WASP IN WALNUT WALRUS SAUCE

BOYSENBERRY BISON BELLY

MACARONI MELON MOSS

MARINARA BAT BANANA

ALLIGATOR BEES AND CHEESE

TAFFY TARRAGON IGUANA

TETRAZZINI ZEBRA KNEES

PRUNE PAPAYA POPPY PARROT

POSSUM PENGUIN PRICKLY PEAR

CATERPILLAR COLA CARROT

GORGONZOLA POLAR BEAR

I cannot imagine anything
more wonderful than these,
filled with succulent ingredients
and guaranteed to please.
Every one is so delicious,
it deserves to win a prize
for the principal proprietor
of **Percy's Perfect Pies.**

COOKIES

LEFTOVERS 4 LIFE

# Deep in Our Refrigerator

Deep in our refrigerator,
there's a special place
for food that's been around awhile . . .
we keep it, just in case.
"It's probably too old to eat,"
my mother likes to say.
"But I don't think it's old enough
for me to throw away."

It stays there for a month or more
to ripen in the cold,
and soon we notice fuzzy clumps
of multicolored mold.
The clumps are larger every day,
we notice this as well,
but mostly what we notice
is a certain special smell.

When finally it all becomes
a nasty mass of slime,
my mother takes it out, and says,
"Apparently, it's time."
She dumps it in the garbage can,
though not without regret,
then fills that space with other food
that's not so ancient yet.

# If Turkeys Thought

If turkeys thought, they'd run away
a week before Thanksgiving Day,
but turkeys can't anticipate,
and so there's turkey on my plate.

## A Piece of Pi
## ("A Pizza the Size of the Sun")

I love pizza. That's why I wrote my poem "A Pizza the Size of the Sun." The word *pizza* begins with the letters PI. I've listed clues for twenty other items that also begin with the letters PI, and after the clue I've given the number of missing letters in the word. How many of these can you name? You may have to put on your thinking cap.

Example: a kind of nut (7)    Answer: PISTACHIO

1. something to rest your head on (4)
2. a baseball player (5)
3. ants sometimes spoil this (4)
4. your smallest finger (4)
5. a cucumber that's been soaked in vinegar (4)
6. a kind of fence (4)
7. something to put in a frame (5)
8. an instrument related to the flute (5)
9. a seagoing robber (4)
10. a common city bird (4)
11. the top of a mountain (6)
12. this has eighty-eight keys (3)
13. you'll find this person in a cockpit (3)
14. a prickly fruit from Hawaii (7)
15. a nasty fish with lots of teeth (5)
16. a ballerina makes this spinning move (7)
17. you get this if you mix red and white (2)
18. early settler of a country (5)
19. a kind of pony (3)
20. you'll find this in a gasoline engine (4)

## Ice Cream and Sandwiches

In "Bleezer's Ice Cream," I created a lot of truly weird and gross confections, and in "Percy's Perfect Pies," I came up with some equally dreadful combinations of ingredients. It's lots of fun to make up your own disgusting recipes. You don't have to restrict yourself to ice cream and pie. Make up recipes for sandwiches, puddings, casseroles, or whatever your heart desires.

Can you make a dish by combining ordinary ingredients that become unappetizing when you mix them together? For example, make a tuna sandwich with chocolate syrup, peanut butter, honey, and pickles. If you ate it, you probably wouldn't like it . . . but then again, maybe you would.

You could even create an entire menu for the worst restaurant in the world. And please feel free to write poems about your concoctions.

## Spaghetti! Spaghetti!

I like spaghetti so much that when I wrote my spaghetti poem I had to say the word *spaghetti* twice. In this puzzle, I've hidden the word *spaghetti* twice. Can you find both strands of spaghetti? They may be spelled left to right, right to left, top to bottom, bottom to top, or on the diagonal either top to bottom or bottom to top. Enjoy!

```
S P T E E H G A P S S P A G H E
S P A G H E T T P P P H S P A T
P S A T E G P A S H G A P S G T
A P A G P S A T S P H G A P S E
G A S P A G H E T I A H G I P H
S P A G G E T T I P A G G T A G
I P I H G H P A G H E S I T G A
T T A G I T E A G P S T T E H P
E H E G T T S T G G T P T H E S
H I T E T H T E T E A G A G T T
G P T H H E H G H I T P P A I E
A S G A G G P G I P A T S P I H
P G P H A A A T E H G A P S H G
S H A P P P S P A G H E T T A I
A P S P S S P A S P A G H E T P
S P A G H E T T A T H E G A P S
```

*Answers on page 192.*

Section Three

# Once They All Believed in Dragons

# The Troll

Be wary of the loathsome troll
that slyly lies in wait
to drag you to his dingy hole
and put you on his plate.

His blood is black and boiling hot,
he gurgles ghastly groans.
He'll cook you in his dinner pot,
your skin, your flesh, your bones.

He'll catch your arms and clutch your legs
and grind you to a pulp,
then swallow you like scrambled eggs—
gobble! gobble! gulp!

So watch your steps when next you go
upon a pleasant stroll,
or you might end in the pit below
as supper for the troll.

# Song of the Gloopy Gloppers

We are Gloppers, gloopy Gloppers,
mucilaginous, gelatinous,
we never fail to find a frail
yet filling form to fatten us,
we ooze about the countryside,
through hamlet and metropolis,
for Gloppers ooze where Gloppers choose,
enveloping the populace.

We are Gloppers, gloopy Gloppers,
unrelenting, irresistible,
what we will do to you is too
distressing to be listable,
we'll ooze into your living room,
your kitchen, and your vestibule,
and in your bed we'll taste your head,
to test if you're digestible.

We are Gloppers, gloopy Gloppers,
globs of undulating Glopper ooze,
you cannot quell our viscid swell,
there is no way to stop our ooze,
for Gloppers are invincible,
unquenchable, unstoppable,
and when we swarm upon *your* form,
we know we'll find you GLOPPABLE!

# Skeleton Parade

The skeletons are out tonight,
They march about the street
With bony bodies, bony heads
And bony hands and feet.

Bony bony bony bones
With nothing in between,
Up and down and all around
They march on Halloween.

# The Wily Wizard Wubaloo

The wily wizard Wubaloo
will wisely waste no words with you,
but simply wink and wave his wings,
which turns you into napkin rings.

# The Snopp on the Sidewalk

It was lying on the sidewalk
like a gray old ragged mop,
but the second that I saw it,
I was sure I'd found the snopp.

It did not move a fiber
of its long and shaggy hair,
as if seeming not to notice
that I stood and watched it there.

At first I thought, "I'll touch it,"
and then I thought, "I won't,"
but when again I thought, "I will,"
the snopp said softly, "Don't."

This startled me so greatly
that I turned to run away,
but as I started down the street,
the snopp called after, "Stay."

I asked, "What do you want of me,
for snopp, I cannot guess?"
The snopp, still never stirring,
only answered me with, "Yes."

I did not understand this
so I tried once more to go,
but I'd barely started homeward
when the snopp said sweetly, "No."

And so I stayed that day and night,
and yes, I stayed a week,
and nevermore in all that time
did either of us speak.

At last I said, "Oh snopp, dear snopp,
I really have to go."
The snopp showed no emotion
as it whispered only, "Oh."

I headed home, not looking back,
afraid to ever stop.
I knew that if I paused but once
I'd never leave the snopp.

But the snopp remains within my mind,
I'm sure it always will—
that strange thing on the sidewalk
that I'm certain lies there still.

# The Ghostly Grocer of Grumble Grove

In Grumble Grove, near Howling Hop,
there stands a nonexistent shop
within which sits, beside his stove,
the ghostly grocer of Grumble Grove.

There on rows of spectral shelves
chickens serenade themselves,
sauces sing to salted butter,
onions weep and melons mutter.

Cornflakes flutter, float on air
with loaves of bread that are not there,
thin spaghettis softly scream
and curdle quarts of quiet cream.

Phantom figs and lettuce specters
dance with cans of fragrant nectars,
sardines saunter down their aisle,
tomatoes march in single file.

A cauliflower poltergeist
juggles apples, thinly sliced,
a sausage skips on ghostly legs
as raisins romp with hard-boiled eggs.

As pea pods play with prickly pears,
the ghostly grocer sits and stares
and watches all within his trove,
that ghostly grocer of Grumble Grove.

# Happy Birthday, Dear Dragon

There were rumbles of strange jubilation
in a dark, subterranean lair,
for the dragon was having a birthday,
and his colleagues were gathering there.
**"HOORAH!"** groaned the trolls and the ogres
as they pelted each other with stones.
**"HOORAH!"** shrieked a sphinx and a griffin,
and the skeletons rattled their bones.

*"HOORAH!"* screamed the queen of the demons.
**"HOORAH!"** boomed a giant. **"REJOICE!"**
"Hoorah!" piped a tiny hobgoblin
in an almost inaudible voice.
*"HOORAH!"* cackled rapturous witches.
"*Hoorahhhhhhh!*" hissed a basilisk too.
Then they howled in cacophonous chorus,
**"HAPPY BIRTHDAY,**
    **DEAR DRAGON,**
        **TO YOU!"**

They whistled, they squawked, they applauded,

as they gleefully brought forth the cake.

**"OH, THANK YOU!"**

he thundered with pleasure

in a bass that made every ear ache.

Then puffing his chest to the fullest,

and taking deliberate aim,

the dragon huffed once at the candles—

**and
the candles
all burst
into
flame!**

# The Gargoyle on the Roof

I am the gargoyle on the roof,
My eyes are fiery red,
My claws are keen and deadly,
And my flinty wings are spread.
I perch atop my domicile
To guard it night and day.
My ears can hear your footfalls
From a thousand miles away.

I am the gargoyle on the roof,
A creature hewn of stone.
My long and lonely vigil
Is the only life I've known.
No sight escapes my tireless gaze,
My nostrils test the air.
If you have cause to enter here,
Take caution, and take care.

Those knaves whose base intention
Is to cause my house distress,
Shall know my wrathful virulence
And feel my cold caress.
I'll strike them and devour them
As an owl devours a mouse . . .
I am the gargoyle on the roof,
And I defend my house.

# The Zubble

The Zubble's mouth is filled with fangs,
it has a tiny nose,
enormous ears, two bloodshot eyes,
and twenty-seven toes.

It has three tails, its hair is green,
and scraggly to the touch,
and so I have decided
that I do not like it much.

# Beware of the Blitter

Beware of the Blitter
that bathes in the bay,
for when its ablutions are done,
it exits the water
and searches for prey . . .
my recommendation is, "Run!"

If ever the Blitter
gets you in its jaws,
it's clear what the Blitter will do.
You'd better beware
of the Blitter, because
it's out to obliterate you.

# The Creature in the Classroom

It appeared inside our classroom

at a quarter after ten,

it gobbled up the blackboard,

three erasers, and a pen.

It gobbled teacher's apple

and it bopped her with the core.

"How dare you!" she responded.

"You must leave us . . . there's the door."

The creature didn't listen
but described an arabesque
as it gobbled all her pencils,
seven notebooks, and her desk.
Teacher stated very calmly,
"Sir! you simply cannot stay.
I'll report you to the principal
unless you go away!"

But the thing continued eating,
it ate paper, swallowed ink.
As it gobbled up our homework,
I believe I saw it wink.
Teacher finally lost her temper.
"OUT!" she shouted at the creature.
The creature hopped beside her
and GLOPP . . . it gobbled teacher.

# I'm Being Abducted by Aliens

I'm being abducted by aliens,
and I'm not enjoying the ride.
They simply appeared in their saucer
and beamed me directly inside.
It's creepy and weird in this saucer,
a strange sort of purplish brown,
I can't tell the floor from the ceiling,
in fact, I may be upside down.

The aliens have odd little bodies,
a cross between melons and eggs.
Their hands end in hundreds of tendrils,
they don't seem to have any legs.
They don't seem to have any noses,
they don't seem to have any eyes,
instead, on their heads are medallions
that keep changing color and size.

They're feeding me gloppy concoctions
that taste even worse than they look.
I guess, since they're totally mouthless,
they don't need to know how to cook.
They haven't revealed where we're going,
or why we are taking this tour.
This unannounced alien abduction
is making me feel insecure.

As we hurtle on through the cosmos,
I'm breathing unbreathable air,
yet all my complaints go unheeded,
my alien abductors don't care.
But now I've a pressing dilemma
that simply cannot be ignored,
I'm dying to go to the bathroom—
they don't seem to have one on board.

# A Place Called Harndegoom

There is a place called Harndegoom,
where dragons freely roam
on every plain and mountaintop,
in every catacomb.
They're fierce, as dragons ought to be,
and ravenous as well,
it's best to keep your distance
from that place where dragons dwell.

But if you're very foolish,
or exceptionally brave,
and do set foot in Harndegoom,
the dragons' last enclave,
you'll soon regret you ever sought
a place where dragons roam . . .
for reasons I need not explain,
you won't be going home.

# Once They All Believed in Dragons

Once they all believed in dragons
When the world was fresh and young,
We were woven into legends,
Tales were told and songs were sung,
We were treated with obeisance,
We were honored, we were feared,
Then one day they stopped believing—
On that day, we disappeared.

Now they say our time is over,
Now they say we've lived our last,
Now we're treated with derision
Where we once ruled unsurpassed.
We must make them all remember,
In some way we must reveal
That our spirit lives forever—
We are dragons! We are real!

• 99

# A Dragon's Lament

I'm tired of being a dragon,
Ferocious and brimming with flame,
The cause of unspeakable terror
When anyone mentions my name.
I'm bored with my bad reputation
For being a miserable brute,
And being routinely expected
To brazenly pillage and loot.

I wish that I weren't repulsive,
Despicable, ruthless, and fierce,
With talons designed to dismember
And fangs finely fashioned to pierce.
I've lost my desire for doing
The deeds any dragon should do,
But since I can't alter my nature,
I guess I'll just terrify you.

# I Am Gooboo

I am Gooboo, who are you?
Can you do what I can do?
I can drink the largest lake,
make the ground beneath me quake.
I can juggle tons of trees,
or a billion bumblebees,
run a hundred thousand miles,
wrestle ninety crocodiles.

There is no one else like me.
I can swim across the sea,
even swallow half the sky
while I hoist a hippo high.
I can dance upon the sun,
dive back down when I am done,
chew the universe in two . . .
I am Gooboo, who are you?

# We're Seven Grubby Goblins

We're seven grubby goblins
You never want to meet,
We fail to wash our faces,
Or clean our filthy feet.
Our hands are always dirty,
We have disheveled hair,
We dress in shabby leggings
And tattered underwear.

We're seven gruesome goblins,
Our habits are uncouth,
We pull each other's teeth out,
Then put back every tooth.
We drink iguana gravy,
We chew polluted prunes,
We dance repugnant dances,
We sing unpleasant tunes.

We're seven grungy goblins,
Determined to displease,
We never blow our noses,
No matter how we sneeze.
We smell like rotten garlic,
We burp around the clock,
This soon should be apparent,
We're moving to your block.

# The Baby Uggs Are Hatching

The baby Uggs are hatching
out of their ugly eggs,
here come their ugly bodies,
here come their ugly legs,
out of their shells they scramble,
fierce and fat and fleet,
back and forth they shamble
on their little ugly feet.

    uggily wuggily zuggily zee
    the baby Uggs are fierce and free,
    uggily wuggily zuggily zay
    the baby Uggs come out today.

The baby Uggs are watching
with their little ugly eyes,
ogling every ugly spot
beneath the ugly skies,
they're lunging and they're lurching
and they're squealing ugly squeals,
the baby Uggs are searching
for their little ugly meals.

    uggily wuggily zuggily zee
    the baby Uggs are fierce and free,
    uggily wuggily zuggily zay
    the baby Uggs come out today.

The baby Uggs are snatching
as they creep along the beach,
gobbling every ugly thing
within their ugly reach,
some gobble down each other
as across the crags they crawl,
and the Uggs that eat their mothers
are the ugliest Uggs of all.

uggily wuggily zuggily zee
the baby Uggs are fierce and free,
uggily wuggily zuggily zay
the baby Uggs come out today.

# The Goblin

There's a goblin as green
As a goblin can be
Who is sitting outside
And is waiting for me.
When he knocked on my door
And said softly, "Come play!"
I answered, "No thank you,
Now please, go away!"

But the goblin as green
As a goblin can be
Is still sitting outside
And is waiting for me.

# The Time Has Come

I think the time has come to throw
the jack-o'-lantern out,
it smells less like a pumpkin
than it does like sauerkraut.
Its expression is peculiar,
it has lost its friendly grin,
it's tilting sort of strangely,
and its cheeks are caving in.

Its forehead is collapsing,
and its eyes are heading south,
its nose is now connected
to the middle of its mouth.
I admit it's been the focus
of some happy family scenes,
but we've had that jack-o'-lantern
for eleven Halloweens.

# The Laugh of the Luffer

The laugh of the Luffer is lovely,
and lively and lilting and long.
The sound of it makes you so happy,
you're likely to burst into song.

The laugh of the Luffer is luscious,
a glorious treat for the ears.
It fills you with feelings of gladness,
and instantly dries all your tears.

The laugh of the Luffer disguises
the Luffer's insidious goal,
and that is to lunge as you listen,
and suddenly swallow you whole.

So listen at length to the laughter,
but if it's too loud, that's your clue,
the Luffer grows closer . . . don't linger,
just leave lest the laugh is on you.

# Activities

## Alien Abduction

In "I'm Being Abducted by Aliens," I describe some very peculiar extraterrestrials that roam the universe in a flying saucer. Take a blank piece of paper, and just from the descriptions in the poem, draw your own outer-space creatures. You might also use your imagination and draw the interior of their spacecraft. There's no right or wrong way . . . it's all up to you. Feel free to invent and illustrate additional aliens that come from beyond our galaxy.

## The Troll and the Snopp

The troll is a creature from traditional folklore. On the other hand, the snopp is entirely my own invention. I wrote poems about both of them, and even though they were meant to be read either silently or aloud, I sometimes set them to familiar tunes and sing them. Both "The Troll" and "The Snopp on the Sidewalk" can be sung to many melodies, including "The Yellow Rose of Texas," "The Marine Hymn" ("From the halls of

Montezuma . . ."), "The Wabash Cannonball," and "America the Beautiful." Can you think of other tunes that will work with these two poems? You can also set any of the other poems in this book to the melodies of songs that you know . . . and, if you really want to be adventurous and creative, you can make up your own melodies.

## Happy Birthday, Dear Dragon

I'm very fond of dragons, perhaps because I was born in a Year of the Dragon, according to the Chinese lunar calendar. That's why I included several dragon poems in this collection. In my poem "Happy Birthday, Dear Dragon," a number of unusual guests are attending the dragon's birthday party. Can you list any other creatures that you might expect to find at a dragon's birthday party . . . and can you imagine what sorts of presents they might give the dragon? There are no right or wrong answers to this—it's just another way to use your imagination.

# Is Traffic Jam Delectable?

# The Average Hippopotamus

The average hippopotamus
is big from top to bottomus,
it travels at a trotamus,
and swims when days are hotamus.

Because it eats a lotamus,
it's practically a yachtamus,
so it's a cinch to spotamus
the average hippopotamus.

# Is Traffic Jam Delectable?

Is traffic jam delectable,
does jelly fish in lakes,
does tree bark make a racket,
does the clamor rattle snakes?
Can salmon scale a mountain,
does a belly laugh a lot,
do carpets nap in flower beds
or on an apricot?

Around my handsome bottleneck,
I wear a railroad tie,
my treasure chest puffs up a bit,
I blink my private eye.
I like to use piano keys
to open locks of hair,
then put a pair of brake shoes on
and dance on debonair.

I hold up my electric shorts
with my banana belt,
then sit upon a toadstool
and watch a tuna melt.
I dive into a car pool,
where I take an onion dip,
then stand aboard the tape deck
and sail my penmanship.

I put my dimes in riverbanks
and take a quarterback,
and when I fix a nothing flat,
I use a lumberjack.
I often wave my second hand
to tell the overtime,
before I pick my bull pen up
to write a silly rhyme.

# Forty Performing Bananas

We're FORTY PERFORMING BANANAS,

in bright yellow slippery skins,

our features are rather appealing,

though we've neither shoulders nor chins,

we cha-cha, fandango, and tango,

we kick and we skip and we hop,

while half of us belt out a ballad,

the rest of us spin like a top.

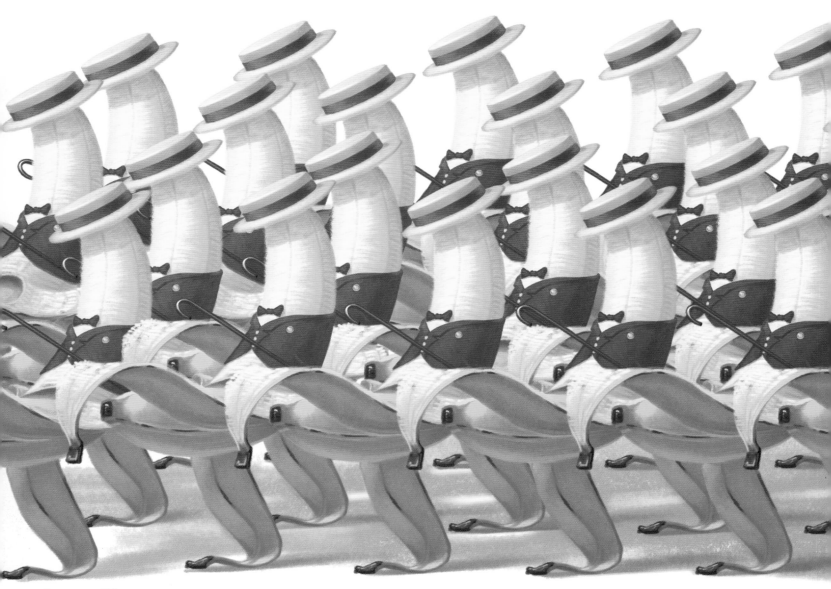

We're FORTY PERFORMING BANANAS,

we mambo, we samba, we waltz,

we dangle and swing from the ceiling,

then turn very slick somersaults,

people drive here in bunches to see us,

our splits earn us worldly renown,

we're FORTY PERFORMING BANANAS,

come see us when you are in town.

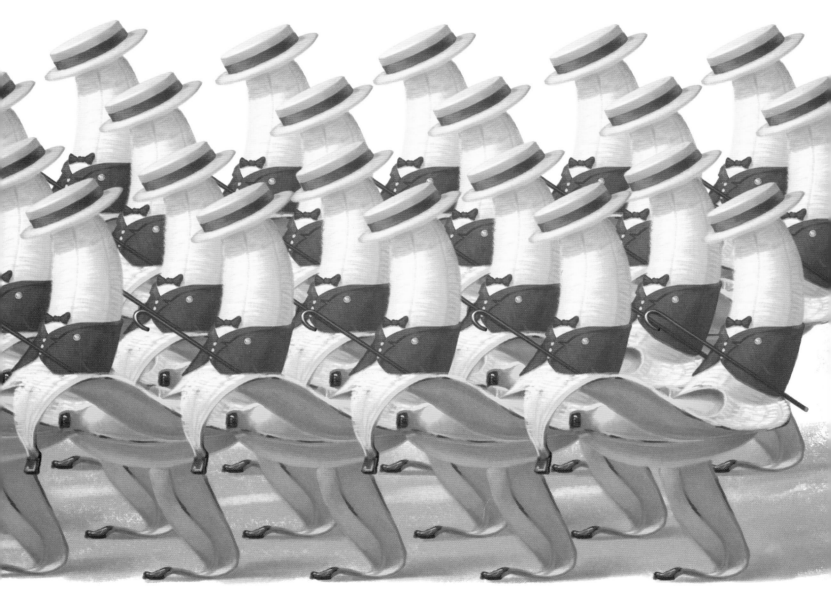

# I Got a Present from My Friend

I got a present from my friend,
which gave me quite a lift.
He sent a comb to me at home —
it was a parting gift.

# Gobble Gobble

When the turkey gobble gobbles,
it is plump and proud and perky,
when our family gobble gobbles,
we are gobbling down the turkey.

# The Wiggling, Wriggling, Jiggling Juggler

The wiggling, wriggling, jiggling juggler
joggles and juggles a jangle of things:
hats and platters that clitter and clatter
and canes and chains and rattles and rings.

Blocks and balls of various sizes
fly from the jiggling juggler's hands.
They twist and twirl, they wobble and whirl,
he calmly catches them where he stands.

Then juggling delicate eggs by the dozen
(they'd certainly splatter if ever they'd fall),
with a mystical twist of his wriggling wrist
the jiggling juggler catches them all.

The wiggling, wriggling, jiggling juggler
joggles and juggles as nobody can.
He makes all things take magical wings—
hooray for the jiggling juggler man!

# Don't Ever Seize a Weasel by the Tail

You should never squeeze a weasel
for you might displease the weasel,
and don't ever seize a weasel by the tail.

Let his tail blow in the breeze;
if you pull it, he will sneeze,
for the weasel's constitution tends to be a little frail.

Yes the weasel wheezes easily;
the weasel freezes easily;
the weasel's tan complexion rather suddenly turns pale.

So don't displease or tease a weasel,
squeeze or freeze or wheeze a weasel
and don't ever seize a weasel by the tail.

# We're Fearless Flying Hot Dogs

We're fearless flying hot dogs,
the famous "Unflappable Five,"
we're mustered in formation
to climb, to dip, to dive,
we spread our wings with relish,
then reach for altitude,
we're aerobatic wieners,
the fastest flying food.

We're fearless flying hot dogs,
we race with flair and style,
then catch up with each other
and soar in single file,
you never saw such daring,
such power and control,
as when we swoop and spiral,
then slide into a roll.

The throngs applaud our antics,
they cheer us long and loud,
there's never a chilly reception,
there's never a sour crowd,
and if we may speak frankly,
we are a thrilling sight,
we're fearless flying hot dogs,
the delicate essence of flight.

# Questions

Can a butcher block and tackle?

May a crossbow tie the knot?

Might a pocket change direction?

Will a talking turkey trot?

Should a station break the ice cream?

Where do balls of fire fly?

Could a clam bake bread and butter?

Does a luncheon counter spy?


Will a hot dog pound the pavement?

Might a snowshoe tree top spin?

Would a mountain pass the time zone?

May the morning fog horn in?

Should a horse show off its rocker?

Will a sitting duck press pants?

Does a cow shed tears of laughter?

Can a teapot belly dance?


Does a sawtooth pick and shovel?

Should a piggy back away?

May a tow truck stop the music?

Would an egg roll overpay?

Could a light foot hold a candle?

Can a kitchen curtain call?

Might a needle point a finger?

Where does running water fall?

# I Put Out the Clock

I put out the clock,

and I wound up the cat.

I took off the lawn,

and I watered my hat.

I lounged on my brother,

and tickled a chair,

then combed my umbrella,

and opened my hair.

I buttoned my supper,

and swallowed my shirt.

I ate my pajamas,

and wore my dessert.

I sat on a tissue,

and sneezed on a pin . . .

I reset the cat,

and I let the clock in.

# Mister Fast Ran Very Slowly

Mister Fast ran very slowly,

Mister Slow ran very fast,

so when they raced each other,

Mister Fast was always last.

They traded names for fun one day,

so things became reversed,

Mister Slow was always second,

Mister Fast was always first.

When they exchanged their names again

to what they were before,

Mister Slow went back to winning,

Mister Fast could win no more.

Although they traded names anew,

it was no longer fun . . .

now neither wins nor loses,

they no longer care to run.

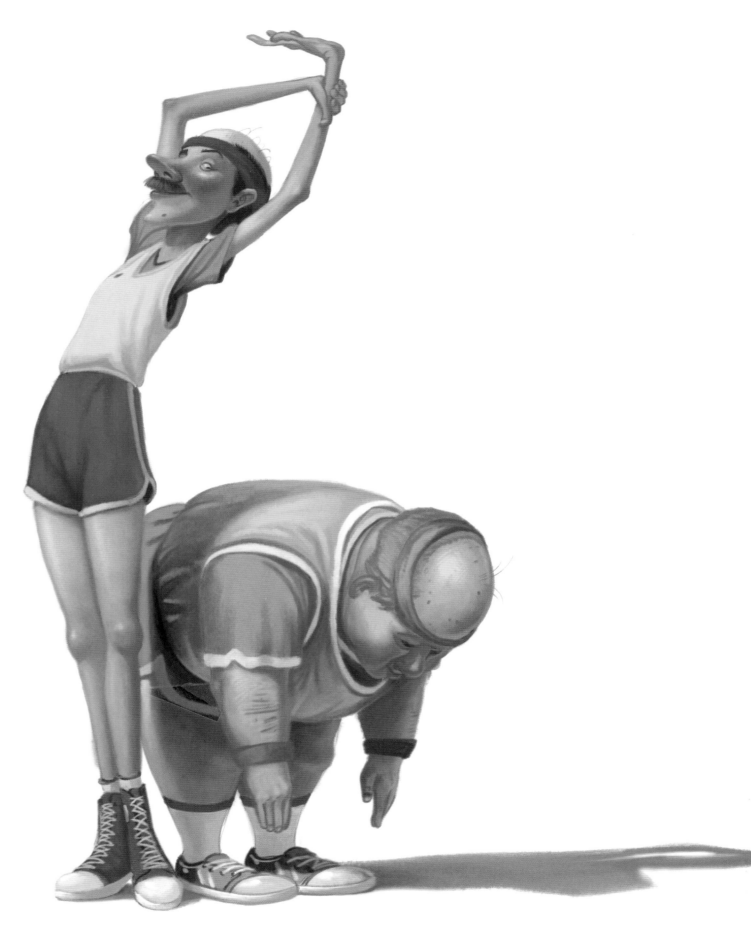

# I Sailed on Half a Ship

I sailed on half a ship
on half the seven seas,
propelled by half a sail
that blew in half a breeze.
I climbed up half a mast
and sighted half a whale
that rose on half a mighty wave
and flourished half a tail.

Each day, with half a hook
and half a rod and reel,
I landed half a fish
that served as half a meal.
I ate off half a plate,
I drank from half a glass,
then mopped up half the starboard deck
and polished half the brass.

When half a year had passed,
as told by half a clock,
I entered half a port
and berthed at half a dock.
Since half my aunts were there
and half my uncles too,
I told them half this half-baked tale
that's half entirely true.

# The Cow

The cow mainly moos as she chooses to moo
and she chooses to moo as she chooses.

She furthermore chews as she chooses to chew
and she chooses to chew as she muses.

If she chooses to moo she may moo to amuse
or may moo just to moo as she chooses.

If she chooses to chew she may moo as she chews
or may chew just to chew as she muses.

# Overheard at the Zoo

Said the kudu to the pudu,
"I have no idea what you do.
Do you do the things that I do,
things that suit a kudu fine?"
"Dearest kudu," said the pudu,
"I'm a pudu, not a kudu,
so I do the things that I do,
things I think are truly mine."

Said the kudu to the pudu,
"I am glad to hear that you do
only things that pudus do do
in a pudu sort of way."
Said the pudu to the kudu,
"Since you do the things that you do,
you are clearly not a pudu—
have a lovely kudu day."

# I Often Repeat Repeat Myself

I often repeat repeat myself,

I often repeat repeat.

I don't I don't know why know why,

I simply know that I I I

am am inclined to say to say

a lot a lot this way this way —

I often repeat repeat myself,

I often repeat repeat.


I often repeat repeat myself,

I often repeat repeat.

My mom my mom gets mad gets mad,

it irritates my dad my dad,

it drives them up a tree tree tree,

that's what they tell they tell me me —

I often repeat repeat myself,

I often repeat repeat.


I often repeat repeat myself,

I often repeat repeat.

It gets me in a jam a jam,

but that's the way I am I am,

in fact I think it's neat it's neat

to to to to repeat repeat —

I often repeat repeat myself,

I often repeat repeat.

# I Gave a Penny to My Friend

I gave a penny to my friend,
he threw it on the ground.
I handed him a nickel,
and he made an awful sound.

He howled for half an hour
when I handed him a dime.
I bestowed him with a quarter,
and he shrieked for twice that time.

In spite of his behavior,
which, admittedly, seems strange,
my friend is not peculiar—
he's just afraid of change.

# Cecil Jessel

My name is Cecil Jessel,
I'm the vampire of the sea.
Captains turn their ships around
as soon as they see me.

No sailor lives who does not dread
the fangs of Cecil Jessel.
They quake in fear when I sail near
upon my red blood vessel.

# If

If a baseball breaks a window,
does it cause the window pain?
If it rains upon a lion,
do the droplets water mane?
If you try to wring a lemon,
can you hear the lemon peal?
If you dream that you are fishing,
is your dream of fishing real?

If an ogre is unhappy,
does it utter giant sighs?
If you catch a booby snooping,
are you sure the booby pries?
If you bleach a bag of garbage,
do you turn the garbage pale?
If you tell a horse a story,
could it be a pony tale?

If you wish to paint a whistle,
will you make the whistle blue?
If you're stuck inside a chimney,
do you suffer from the flue?
If you sketch an escalator,
did you practice drawing stairs?
If you separate two rabbits,
are you really splitting hares?

If you're filling in a doughnut,
do you make the doughnut whole?
If you're posing as a muffin,
are you acting out a roll?
If your conversation sparkles,
do you thank your diamond mind?
If you're followed by a grizzly,
do you have a bear behind?

# It's Hot, Hot, Hot

"It's hot, hot, hot," the rabbit said,
"and truly, that's too bad.
This morning I was happy,
but I'm starting to get mad.

"I've lost my sense of humor,
and there's nothing I find funny.
This weather's changed my attitude—
I'm now a hot cross bunny."

## Stinky Pinky

All the poems in this section involve some sort of wordplay. I enjoy playing word games and have invented a number of my own. One of my favorite traditional word games, though, is called Stinky Pinky. I'll give you a two-word definition, and you have to come up with two rhyming words that satisfy the definition. In this version, all the words in the answers are words of one syllable. Some of them are tricky, but if you think hard, you should be able to solve them all. After you've solved these, try making up your own—it's fun.

**Example:** NASTY RULER      **Answer:** MEAN QUEEN

1. **RODENT HOME**
2. **BEIGE CONTAINER**
3. **MOIST LIGHT**
4. **SPICY BOAT**
5. **TINY SPHERE**
6. **SHOWER ACHE**
7. **LARGE SWINE**
8. **IMITATION SERPENT**
9. **SICK MOUNTAIN**
10. **SCARLET ROLL**
11. **STRANGE WHISKERS**
12. **SPHERICAL DOG**
13. **UNFAMILIAR COINS**
14. **UNUSUAL RABBIT**
15. **OBESE FELINE**
16. **SAD FOOTWEAR**
17. **UTENSIL SONG**
18. **LARGE BOX**

## Titles around a Wheel

I've hidden the titles of two of the poems from this section around a wheel. Start with any letter, then skip over the next letter to the one after it. Continue by using **every other letter.** Ignore spaces between words. The titles may go in the same direction or in opposite directions, so it may take you a bit of time to find both of them. You may end up using some letters more than once. If you have no luck with your starting letter, then try another one. I know that you'll solve this if you really try.

## Circles, Triangles, and Rectangles

I was typing up the titles of some of the poems in this book when I accidentally hit the wrong key. From out of nowhere, a flurry of colored circles, triangles, and rectangles appeared, covering much of what I had just typed. I looked at this for a while and noticed that with a bit of effort I could still figure out all the titles. Can you?

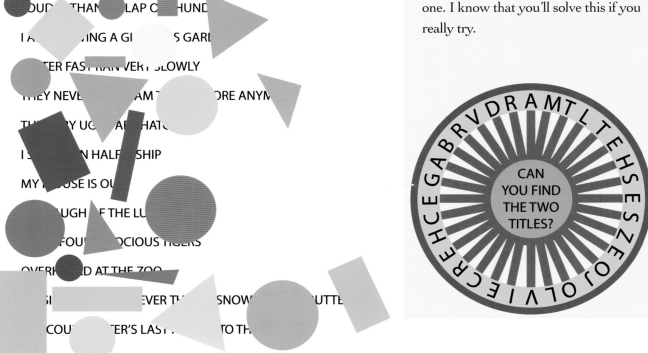

*Answers on pages 192–193.*

Section Five

# There Was
# a Little Poet

# There Was a Little Poet

There was a little poet
with a little silver pen,
who liked to write a little,
every little now and then.
He took a little journey
to a little mountain stream,
and there he took a little nap
and dreamed a little dream.

He dreamed of little dragons,
and he dreamed of little kings,
he dreamed of little elephants
with little golden wings.
He woke a little later
and he thought a little while,
then wrote a book of little rhymes
and smiled a little smile.

# I Am Growing a Glorious Garden

I am growing a glorious garden,
resplendent with trumpets and flutes,
I am pruning euphonium bushes,
I am watering piccolo shoots,
my tubas and tambourines flourish,
surrounded by saxophone reeds,
I am planting trombones and pianos,
and sowing sweet sousaphone seeds.

I have cymbals galore in my garden,
staid oboes in orderly rows,
there are flowering fifes and violas
in the glade where the glockenspiel grows,
there are gongs and guitars in abundance,
there are violins high on the vine,
and an arbor of harps by the bower
where the cellos and clarinets twine.

My bassoons are beginning to blossom,
as my zithers and mandolins bloom,
my castanets happily chatter,
my kettledrums merrily boom,
the banjos that branch by the bugles
play counterpoint with a kazoo,
come visit my glorious garden
and hear it play music for you.

# Awful Ogre Rises

My rattlesnake awakens me,
I swat its scaly head.
My buzzard pecks my belly
Till I fling it from the bed.
My rats attack me as I rise
But scatter when I roar.
I boot my sweet tarantula
Across the stony floor.

I tickle my piranha,
Who rewards me with a bite,
Then disengage the leeches
That besiege me overnight.
I flick aside the lizard
Clinging grimly to my chin,
And now I feel I'm ready
For my morning to begin.

# Be Glad
# Your Nose
# Is on Your Face

Be glad your nose is on your face,

not pasted on some other place,

for if it were where it is not,

you might dislike your nose a lot.

Imagine if your precious nose

were sandwiched in between your toes,

that clearly would not be a treat,

for you'd be forced to smell your feet.

Your nose would be a source of dread

were it attached atop your head,

it soon would drive you to despair,

forever tickled by your hair.

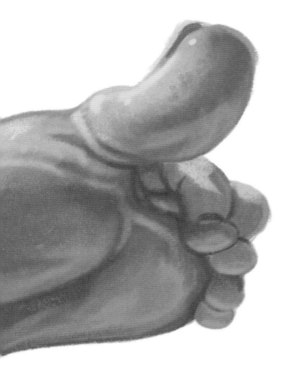

Within your ear, your nose would be
an absolute catastrophe,
for when you were obliged to sneeze,
your brain would rattle from the breeze.

Your nose, instead, through thick and thin,
remains between your eyes and chin,
not pasted on some other place—
be glad your nose is on your face!

# Mold, Mold

Mold, mold,
marvelous mold,
alluring to look at,
enthralling to hold,
you are so delightful
I can't help but smile
when I nuzzle a smidgen
of mold for awhile.

Slime, slime,
savory slime,
you're luscious and succulent
any old time,
there's hardly a thing
that is nearly as grand
as a dollop of slime
in the palm of my hand.

Some think you are miserable
manners of muck,
they can't stand to see you,
you make them say, "Yuck!"
But I think you're fetching,
beguiling and fine,
mold, you are glorious,
slime, you're divine.

# Dixxer's Excellent Elixir

Dexter Dixxer mixed elixir
in his quick elixir mixer.
"It's an excellent elixir,"
Dexter boasted, "very fine
for afflictions which assail you,
aches which irritate and ail you,
guaranteed to rarely fail you,
only nineteen ninety-nine!"

His elixir tasted icky,
it was fishy, squishy, sticky,
just to swallow it was tricky,
and I tried to spit it out.
But too late! My tongue already
started turning to spaghetti,
and my hair was red confetti
with a touch of sauerkraut.

I grew feathers on my belly,
all my fingers felt like jelly,
then my feet got really smelly,
and my ears were green as limes.
I was squawking, I was squealing,
and I had a sinking feeling,
so I jumped up to the ceiling,
and I sneezed eleven times.

I was yipping, I was yapping,
as my kneecaps started clapping,
then my earlobes started flapping,
and my nose turned violet.
So I ran and told my mother,
"This elixir's like no other!"
Now I share it with my brother—
it's the best elixir yet!

# Sally, Sally

Sally, Sally, you're so silly.
What are you about—
sitting on a water lily,
calling to a trout?

Silly Sally, how you dally.
Why are you so fond
of your lily, silly Sally,
on the lily pond?

# Bobbing for Apples

Watch us bobbing for an apple,
For an apple apple apple,
But no apple apple apple,
Not an apple can I get.

Oh I cannot catch an apple,
Not one apple apple apple.
Though my sister got an apple,
All I got was soaking wet.

# Euphonica Jarre

Euphonica Jarre has a voice that's bizarre,
but Euphonica warbles all day,
as windowpanes shatter and chefs spoil the batter
and mannequins moan with dismay.

Mighty ships run aground at her horrible sound,
pretty pictures fall out of their frames,
trees drop off their branches,
rocks start avalanches,
and flower beds burst into flames.

When she opens her mouth, even eagles head south,
little fish truly wish they could drown,
the buzzards all hover, as tigers take cover,
and rats pack their bags and leave town.

Milk turns into butter and butterflies mutter
and bees look for something to sting,
pigs peel off their skins, a tornado begins
when Euphonica Jarre starts to sing.

# The Ball Game Is Over

The ball game is over,
And here is the score—
They got ninety-seven,
We got ninety-four.

Baseball is fun,
But it gives me the blues
To score ninety-four
And still manage to lose.

# My Sister Would Never Throw Snowballs at Butterflies

My sister would never throw snowballs at butterflies,

lately, they've not been around,

and certainly not at a dragon or unicorn,

both are infrequently found.

She cannot throw any at fishes or porpoises,

we are quite far from the sea,

and never, no, never at tigers or elephants,

she only throws them at me.

# You're a Mess

"You're a mess," laughed my mother,
"you've twigs in your hair.
There's dirt on your face,
and there's mud everywhere.

"I hardly can tell
you're my own little son.
You're a mess, so I guess
you had plenty of fun."

# We're Shaking Maracas

We're shaking maracas
And beating on drums,
We're tapping on tables
With fingers and thumbs.
We jingle our bells,
And we play tambourines,
We rattle our bottles
Of buttons and beans.

We're blowing our whistles
And tooting kazoos,
We're clanging our cymbals
As loud as we choose.
We stomp up and down
On the floor with our feet. . . .
We love making music,
The sound is so sweet.

# They Never Send Sam to the Store Anymore

The day they sent Sam to the grocery store

to purchase a carton of eggs,

he brought back a pear with a pearl in its core,

and a leopard with lavender legs.

He returned with an elephant small as a mouse,

a baseball that bounces a mile,

a little tame dragon that heats up the house,

and a lantern that lights when they smile.

Sam brought them a snowball that never feels cold,

a gossamer carpet that flies,

a salmon of silver, a grackle of gold,

and an ermine with emerald eyes.

They never send Sam to the store anymore,

no matter how often he begs,

for he brought back a dodo that danced on the floor,

but he didn't bring home any eggs.

# I Only Got One Valentine

I only got one valentine,
and *that* was signed

## Love,
## Frankenstein

# Sometimes

Sometimes I simply have to cry,
I don't know why,
I don't know why.
There's really nothing very wrong,
I probably should sing a song
or run around and make some noise
or sit and tinker with my toys
or pop a couple of balloons
or play a game or watch cartoons,
but I'm feeling sad,
though I don't know why,
and all I want to do is cry.

# A Snowflake Fell

A snowflake fell into my hand,
a tiny, fragile gem,
a frosty crystal flowerlet
with petals, but no stem.

I wondered at the beauty
of its intricate design,
I breathed, the snowflake vanished,
but for moments, it was mine.

# A Million Candles

A million candles fill the night,
they glister in the dark,
and though by day they hide their glow,
now each displays its spark.

Amidst them all, there is one light
that has a special shine,
and that's the one whose name I know . . .
I think that it knows mine.

# One Day in Seattle

One day in Seattle
I sat by the Sound.
The salmon were jumping,
the birds flew around.
The seagulls were begging
for morsels of bread,
as ominous clouds
gathered high overhead.

A ferry went out,
and a ferry came in.
It started to rain,
I got soaked to my skin.
Seattle is lovely,
but I cannot lie—
without an umbrella
it's hard to stay dry.

# The Court Jester's Last Report to the King

Oh sire! My sire! your castle's on fire,

I fear it's about to explode,

a hideous lizard has eaten the wizard,

the prince has turned into a toad.


Oh sire! Good sire! there's woe in the shire,

fierce trolls are arriving in force,

there are pirates in port, monstrous ogres at court,

and a dragon has melted your horse.


Oh sire! Great sire! the tidings are dire,

a giant has trampled the school,

your army has fled, there are bees in your bed

and your nose has come off . . . . . . APRIL FOOL!

# Lumpy Is My Friend

Lumpy likes to pick his nose,
then wipe his fingers on my clothes.
It doesn't matter, I suppose,
for Lumpy is my friend.

He hides my shoes, he steals my hats,
he pulls the tails of dogs and cats,
oh, Lumpy is the brat of brats,
still, Lumpy is my friend.

Lumpy thinks it's lots of fun
to shoot me with his water gun
and trip me when I try to run,
still, Lumpy is my friend.

He stuffs my pockets full of rice
and down my back slips chunks of ice,
I know that Lumpy isn't nice,
but Lumpy is my friend.

# Louder Than a Clap of Thunder!

Louder than a clap of thunder,
louder than an eagle screams,
louder than a dragon blunders,
or a dozen football teams,
louder than a four-alarmer,
or a rushing waterfall,
louder than a knight in armor
jumping from a ten-foot wall.

Louder than an earthquake rumbles,
louder than a tidal wave,
louder than an ogre grumbles
as he stumbles through his cave,
louder than stampeding cattle,
louder than a cannon roars,
louder than a giant's rattle,
*that's* how loud my father *SNORES!*

# Singing Christmas Carols

On Christmas Eve we bundle up
and go out caroling,
our neighbors shut their windows
when they hear my family sing.

*My* voice is very beautiful,
I sing just like a bird,
but everybody drowns me out
so I am barely heard.

Dad sings like a buffalo
and Mother like a moose,
my sister sounds like breaking glass,
my brother like a goose.

Some people come and greet us,
they bring cookies on a tray,
I think they give us cookies
just to make us go away.

Though our singing sounds so sour
it sends shivers down my spine,
when we're caroling together
there's no family sweet as mine.

# I Peered in a Mirror

I peered in a mirror,
the mirror fell down.
I glanced at my shadow,
it sped out of town.

I watched my reflection
swim off in the sea—
there's something peculiar
today about me.

# I Wash My Shadow Weekly

I wash my shadow weekly
to make my shadow shine,
so there's no other shadow
as immaculate as mine.
I scrub it with detergent,
and so when I am done,
my shadow is impeccable
and glistens in the sun.

My neighbors are astonished
to see me stroll about.
"Your shadow's simply spotless,"
they clamorously shout.
I wonder if my shadow
might wind up cleaner still
if I took a bath or shower—
perhaps someday I will.

# I Wished into a Wishing Well

I wished into a wishing well,
my wishes were in vain.
I tried to catch a rainbow,
but it vanished like the rain.

I dug for buried treasure
till my shovel came apart.
I heard a rhyme inside my head,
and now it's in my heart.

## The Ball Game Is Over

I've made a list of twenty two-word phrases, most of which don't seem to mean anything. However, each two-word pair rhymes with a common baseball term. For example, the

phrase THIRST RACE rhymes with FIRST BASE and WINCH KIT rhymes with PINCH HIT. Now let's see if you can hit a COMB SUN.

1. NINE FIVE
2. TOP SKY
3. FATTER PUP
4. SHOW NERVE
5. BITE YIELD
6. BIRD LACE
7. BUBBLE DAY
8. COURT FLOP
9. MILD WITCH
10. FOAM SLATE
11. BIKE FLEA
12. CHUCKLE FALL
13. BLUE TROUT
14. MALL STORE
15. OWL GRIP
16. RIPPLE TRAY
17. SOUND WALL
18. TOE KNITTER
19. STITCHING ROACH
20. CANNED HAM

# Activities

## Louder Than a Clap of Thunder

The poem "Louder Than a Clap of Thunder!" is based on my father, who was the loudest snorer that I've ever heard. I compare his snoring to many **loud** sounds, such as an earthquake, a tidal wave, and a cattle stampede. Try making a list of all the *soft* sounds you can think of, such as an elf's whisper, the whirring of a tiny fan, or the buzz of the world's smallest bee. You might even write a poem about these things. You can also make lists about big things and small things, hot things and cold things, new things and old things, and so on. As always, use your imagination.

## One Hundred Hearts

The last poem in this book is "I Wished into a Wishing Well," and the last word in the last poem is *heart*. Here are a hundred hearts, all similar to each other . . . but only two are exactly alike. Can you find those two in less than five minutes?

**All the poems and activities in this book come to you from the bottom of my heart.**

—J. P.

*Answers on page 193.*

# Index to Titles

# Index to First Lines

# Answers for Activities

## HERE COME THE ELEPHANTS, *p. 41*

| | | | | | |
|---|---|---|---|---|---|
| ALEE | HEAP | LEAP | PATE | PETAL | TALE |
| ANTE | HEEL | LENT | PATH | PLAN | TAPE |
| ELAN | HELP | NAPE | PEAL | PLANE | TEAL |
| ELATE | LANE | NEAP | PEEL | PLANT | TEEN |
| HALE | LATE | NEAT | PEEN | PLAT | THAN |
| HALT | LATH | PANE | PELT | PLATE | THANE |
| HATE | LATHE | PANEL | PENAL | PLEA | THEE |
| HEAL | LEAN | PANT | PENT | PLEAT | |

There may be other words, but these are the ones I found on my first try.

## A PIECE OF PI, *p. 75*

1. PILLOW
2. PITCHER
3. PICNIC
4. PINKIE
5. PICKLE
6. PICKET
7. PICTURE
8. PICCOLO
9. PIRATE
10. PIGEON
11. PINNACLE
12. PIANO
13. PILOT
14. PINEAPPLE
15. PIRANHA
16. PIROUETTE
17. PINK
18. PIONEER
19. PINTO
20. PISTON

## SPAGHETTI! SPAGHETTI!, *p. 7*

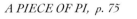

## STINKY PINKY, *p. 143*

1. MOUSE HOUSE
2. TAN CAN
3. DAMP LAMP
4. HOT YACHT
5. SMALL BALL
6. RAIN PAIN
7. BIG PIG
8. FAKE SNAKE
9. ILL HILL
10. RED BREAD
11. WEIRD BEARD
12. ROUND HOUND
13. STRANGE CHANGE
14. RARE HARE
15. FAT CAT
16. BLUE SHOE
17. SPOON TUNE
18. GREAT CRATE

*CIRCLES, TRIANGLES, AND RECTANGLES, p. 143*

"Louder Than a Clap of Thunder"
"I Am Growing a Glorious Garden"
"Mister Fast Ran Very Slowly"
"They Never Send Sam to the
    Store Anymore"

"The Baby Uggs Are Hatching"
"I Sailed on Half a Ship"
"My Mouse Is Out"
"The Laugh of the Luffer"
"We're Four Ferocious Tigers"

"Overheard at the Zoo"
"My Sister Would Never Throw Snowballs
    at Butterflies"
"The Court Jester's Last Report to the King"

*TITLES AROUND A WHEEL , p. 143*

CECIL JESSEL begins here and proceeds counterclockwise, using every other letter.

OVERHEARD AT THE ZOO begins here and proceeds clockwise, using every other letter.

*THE BALL GAME IS OVER , p. 185*

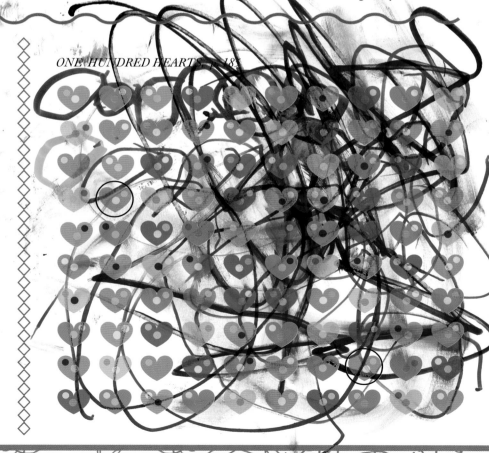

ONE HUNDRED HEARTS , 185

1. LINE DRIVE
2. POP FLY
3. BATTER UP
4. SLOW CURVE
5. RIGHT FIELD
6. THIRD BASE
7. DOUBLE PLAY
8. SHORT HOP
9. WILD PITCH
10. HOME PLATE
11. STRIKE THREE
12. KNUCKLE BALL
13. TWO OUT
14. BALL FOUR
15. FOUL TIP
16. TRIPLE PLAY
17. GROUND BALL
18. NO HITTER
19. PITCHING COACH
20. GRAND SLAM

## The following poems first appeared in book form in the titles listed below:

*Awful Ogre's Awful Day* (Greenwillow Books, 2001): "Awful Ogre Rises," "Awful Ogre's Breakfast"

*The Baby Uggs Are Hatching* (Greenwillow Books, 1982): "The Baby Uggs Are Hatching," "The Creature in the Classroom"

*Behold the Bold Umbrellaphant* (Greenwillow Books, 2006): "The Ballpoint Penguins," "The Clocktopus," "The Solitary Spatuloon"

*Beneath a Blue Umbrella* (Greenwillow Books, 1990): "Oh Farmer, Poor Farmer," "Eleven Yellow Monkeys"

*Circus* (Macmillan, 1974): "Here Come the Elephants," "The Wiggling, Wriggling, Jiggling Juggler"

*The Dragons Are Singing Tonight* (Greenwillow Books, 1993): "A Dragon's Lament," "Once They All Believed in Dragons"

*The Frogs Wore Red Suspenders* (Greenwillow Books, 2002): "The Frogs Wore Red Suspenders," "One Day in Seattle"

*The Gargoyle on the Roof* (Greenwillow Books, 1999): "The Gargoyle on the Roof"

*Ghost Poems*, Daisy Wallace, ed. (Holiday House, 1979): "The Ghostly Grocer of Grumble Grove"

*Good Sports* (Alfred A. Knopf, 2007): "The Ball Game Is Over"

*If Not for the Cat* (Greenwillow Books, 2004): "Boneless, Translucent," "If Not for the Cat"

*In Aunt Giraffe's Green Garden* (Greenwillow Books, 2007): "Sally, Sally," "There Was a Little Poet"

*It's Christmas* (Greenwillow Books, 1981): "Singing Christmas Carols"

*It's Halloween* (Greenwillow Books, 1977): "Bobbing for Apples," "The Goblin," "Skeleton Parade"

*It's Raining Pigs & Noodles* (Greenwillow Books, 2000): "Deep in Our Refrigerator," "Is Traffic Jam Delectable?" "I'm Being Abducted by Aliens," "Percy's Perfect Pies," "Questions," "The Time Has Come," "Worm Puree"

*It's Snowing! It's Snowing!* (Greenwillow Books, 1984): "A Snowflake Fell," "My Sister Would Never Throw Snowballs at Butterflies"

*It's Thanksgiving* (Greenwillow Books, 1982): "Gobble Gobble," "If Turkeys Thought"

*It's Valentine's Day* (Greenwillow Books, 1983): "I Only Got One Valentine"

*Monday's Troll* (Greenwillow Books, 1996): "Chitterchat," "We're Seven Grubby Goblins"

*My Dog May Be a Genius* (Greenwillow Books, 2008): "The Average Hippopotamus," "I Am Gooboo," "I Peered in a Mirror," "I Wished into a Wishing Well," "I'm Dancing with My Elephants," "The Laugh of the Luffer," "My Dog May Be a Genius," "My Mouse Is Out," "Song of the Lizard Lovers"

*My Parents Think I'm Sleeping* (Greenwillow Books, 1985): "A Million Candles"

*The New Kid on the Block* (Greenwillow Books, 1984): "Ballad of a Boneless Chicken," "Bleezer's Ice Cream," "Be Glad Your Nose Is on Your Face," "Euphonica Jarre," "Forty Performing Bananas," "Happy Birthday, Dear Dragon," "Louder Than a Clap of Thunder!" "My Dog, He Is an Ugly Dog," "My Mother Says I'm Sickening," "Song of the Gloopy Gloppers"

*Nightmares: Poems to Trouble Your Sleep* (Greenwillow Books, 1976): "The Troll"

*A Pizza the Size of the Sun* (Greenwillow Books, 1996): "Dixxer's Excellent Elixir," "Eyeballs for Sale!" "I Often Repeat Repeat Myself," "I Sailed on Half a Ship," "If," "It's Hard to Be an Elephant," "A Pizza the Size of the Sun," "Rat for Lunch!"

*The Queen of Eene* (Greenwillow Books, 1978): "Herbert Glerbett," "Pumberly Pott's Unpredictable Niece"

*Rainy, Rainy Saturday* (Greenwillow Books, 1980): "Sometimes," "Spaghetti! Spaghetti!"

*Ride a Purple Pelican* (Greenwillow Books, 1986): "Early One Morning on Featherbed Lane"

*Rolling Harvey Down the Hill* (Greenwillow Books, 1980): "Lumpy Is My Friend," "Willie Ate a Worm"

*Scranimals* (Greenwillow Books, 2002): "The Detested Radishark," "Oh Sleek Bananaconda"

*The Sheriff of Rottenshot* (Greenwillow Books, 1982): "The Court Jester's Last Report to the King"

*The Snopp on the Sidewalk* (Greenwillow Books, 1977): "The Frummick and the Frelly," "The Snopp on the Sidewalk"

*Something Big Has Been Here* (Greenwillow Books, 1990): "Hello! How Are You? I Am Fine!" "I Am Growing a Glorious Garden," "I Saw a Brontosaurus," "Mold, Mold," "My Mother Made a Meat Loaf," "They Never Send Sam to the Store Anymore," "We're Fearless Flying Hot Dogs," "We're Four Ferocious Tigers"

*Tyrannosaurus Was a Beast: Dinosaur Poems* (Greenwillow Books, 1988): "Brachiosaurus," "Clankity Clankity"

*What a Day It Was at School!* (Greenwillow Books, 2006): "In the Cafeteria," "We're Shaking Maracas"

*Zoo Doings* (Greenwillow Books, 1983): "The Armadillo," "The Cow," "Don't Ever Seize a Weasel by the Tail," "The Egg"

The following poems are original to this collection: "Beware of the Blitter," "Cecil Jessel," "I Gave a Penny to My Friend," "I Got a Present from My Friend," "I Put Out the Clock," "I Wash My Shadow Weekly," "It's Hot, Hot, Hot," "Mister Fast Ran Very Slowly," "My Dog in Most Ways," "My Frog Does Not Waste Precious Time," "Overheard at the Zoo," "A Place Called Harndegoom," "The Wily Wizard Wubaloo," "You're a Mess," "The Zubble"